# Goes to the Beach

by Deborah Bodin Cohen • illustrations by CB Decker

Based on the character by Claudia Carlson

Inspired by Jacqueline Goldman and her longtime vision to produce
a children's book about the miraculous, lifesaving work of Magen David Adom.

For Yosef Tzvi and Hillel—DBC

To Elianna and Isabel, two great rescuers!—CBD

The publisher greatly acknowledges the following sources of photographs: P 32 Shutterstock: Aria Armoko (thank you note); Dolores M. Harvey (hospital); SvetaZi (doctor hand); artaxerxes_longhand (Tiberias). All other photos used by permission from American Friends of Magen David Adom.

Apples & Honey Press
An Imprint of Behrman House Publishers
Millburn, New Jersey 07041
www.applesandhoneypress.com

ISBN 978-1-68115-667-5

Copyright © 2025 Behrman House

All rights reserved. No part of this publication may be translated, reproduced, stored in a retrieval system or transmitted, in any form or by any means, electronic, mechanical, photocopying, recording or otherwise, for any purpose, without express written permission from the publishers. The characters in this book are under trademark by American Friends of Magen David Adom.

Library of Congress Cataloging-in-Publication Data

Names: Cohen, Deborah Bodin, 1968- author. | Decker, CB, illustrator.
Title: Avi the ambulance goes to the beach / by Deborah Bodin Cohen ; illustrated by CB Decker.

Description: Millburn, New Jersey : Apples & Honey Press, an imprint of Behrman House Publishers, 2025. | Audience term: Children | Audience: Ages 4-7. | Audience: Grades K-1. | Summary: Avi the Ambulance meets Noah, a boat who is also an ambulance, and learns how someone so different can share the same important role.
Identifiers: LCCN 2024030911 | ISBN 9781681156675 (paperback)
Subjects: CYAC: Ambulances—Fiction. | Motorboats—Fiction. | Emergency vehicles—Fiction. | Rescue work—Fiction. | Jews—Israel—Fiction. | Israel—Fiction. | LCGFT: Picture books.
Classification: LCC PZ7.C6623 Av 2025 | DDC [E]—dc23
LC record available at https://lccn.loc.gov/2024030911

Edited by Dena Neusner
Art direction by Lindsey Mauriello and Dena Neusner
Printed in China

1 3 5 7 9 8 6 4 2

In a garage in Jerusalem lived a family of ambulances. They traveled over land and through the air to save lives.

Avi was the youngest and one of the smallest ambulances. He had four shiny wheels that took him everywhere, safely and quickly.

On roads. Zoom.

Zack the medic inspected Avi to make sure all his parts were in tip-top shape.

Oh no! Avi's shiny wheels did not pass inspection.

Zack said, "I'll put more air in your tires."
**Buzzzz**. Avi giggled. "That tickles."

After inspection, Zack surprised Avi. "We are going to the beach. My friend Esti invited us to meet her new ambulance partner."

Avi loved trips!
Avi loved the beach!

And he loved new friends even more!
Avi revved up his engine, ready to go.

Vrooom!

Avi wound his way through Jerusalem's busy streets.
**Zoom, zoom, zoom.**

Avi coasted down the hill toward Tel Aviv.
**Whoosh!**

Avi whizzed toward Haifa, then turned east toward Tiberias.
**Zip, zip, zip!**

In Tiberias, Esti greeted Zack and patted Avi's hood.
Avi rotated his headlights and looked across the parking lot and then at the beach. "Where's your new ambulance partner?" he asked.

Esti said, "You won't find Noah on land. He is a boat."

She pointed to a yellow motorboat docked at the pier.

"A boat can't be an ambulance!" said Avi.

"Why not?" asked Esti.

"A boat does not have wheels!" said Avi.

"Hila the Helicopter doesn't have wheels," said Zack.
"But Hila has rotor blades. They go *buzz*!" said Avi.
"How can a boat bring people to the hospital?"
"Noah is very much an ambulance," said Esti. "Come, let me introduce you!"

"Noah, meet Avi," said Esti. "He's an ambulance just like you."
"Ahoy!" said Noah with a grin.

Avi saw flashing lights and a siren on Noah's roof and a red star on his side.

Why does a boat need a siren? Avi wondered. There are no roads or traffic lights in the water.

Suddenly, somebody cried, "I need *heeelp!*"
Avi scanned the beach and then the water.
A boy in a rowboat had caught a fish. It was so big that he couldn't reel it in.

Oh no! The fish pulled the boy right into the water! *Kerplunk!*

Avi wanted to help, but he couldn't swim.
"Help!" cried the boy, splashing around.
"Help!" cried his grandfather in the rowboat.

"Okay, Noah, let's get to work!" called Esti. She jumped onto Noah's deck. Noah revved his engine.

*Vroom!*
He took off through the water.

Esti threw a life preserver into the water. The boy grabbed the ring, and Esti used the rope to pull him onto Noah's deck.

Then Noah sped back to the dock, lights flashing and siren wailing.

*Woooo-woooo!*

All the other boats moved out of the way.

After Noah docked, Zack and Esti helped the boy climb onto the pier.

With their help, he hopped over to Avi.
"Noah, thank you for rescuing me!" he called out.

"Avi, now it's your turn to help," said Zack. "Let's take our patient to the hospital to be sure his ankle is okay."

Avi put on his siren. *WOOOO-WOOOO!*
He sped toward the hospital. *Vroom!*

"Noah is a very helpful ambulance, even if he doesn't have wheels," said Zack.

"I agree!" said Avi. "And Noah does have one very important wheel: his life preserver."

# The Lifesaving Work of Magen David Adom

*Avi the Ambulance Goes to the Beach* is based on the real work of Magen David Adom, Israel's ambulance, blood-services, and disaster-relief organization, whose emergency medical first responders serve the country's more than nine million people.

In 2019, Magen David Adom launched a marine rescue ambulance for Lake Kinneret in Tiberias. Since then, MDA has increased the fleet by adding medical Jet Skis to its Kinneret operations and an additional boat that is used in the Red Sea and is based in Eilat.

The story highlights Jewish values such as *piku'ach nefesh*, the importance of saving lives, and *g'vurah*, heroism. In addition, just as there are a variety of land, air, and water ambulances, we can help one another in different ways, even when we have different abilities. Avi practices *hakarat hatov*, expressing appreciation to others, when he acknowledges the ways Noah is a helpful ambulance.

More than thirty thousand professionals and volunteers help save lives at MDA. Learn more at MagenDavidAdom.org.

**light bar:** Lights that are on top of an ambulance. When turned on, they signal others that the ambulance is on an urgent mission.

**bow:** The most forward part of the ship when in motion. The front of this boat opens for easy loading and unloading of equipment and patients.

**motor:** The system that allows the boat to drive on water quickly. It includes an engine and a propeller.

**logo:** The Magen David Adom symbol and name, in Hebrew and English.

**hull:** The watertight body of the boat that keeps it afloat and protects it from damage.

## Vocabulary

 **ambulance:** A special vehicle used to move hurt or sick people to a hospital. Avi is an ambulance.

 **life preserver:** An inflatable ring made of strong material to keep someone afloat in the water.

 **diversity:** A range of differences. MDA's rescue vehicles and medics may have different talents, but they all work to help others.

 **marine rescue ambulance:** A special boat used to rescue people in the water and bring them back to shore. Noah is a marine rescue ambulance.

 *g'vurah:* Heroism. Jewish tradition challenges us to stand up, be brave, and do what is good for humanity.

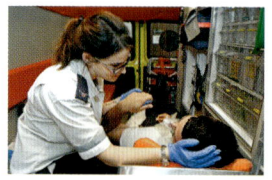 **medic:** A person trained to help take care of hurt or sick people. Zack and Esti are medics.

 *hakarat hatov:* Expressing appreciation to others.

 **medical helicopter:** A special helicopter used to quickly transport people to a hospital. Hila is a medical helicopter.

 **hospital:** A building where doctors, nurses, and others take care of hurt or sick people.

 *piku'ach nefesh:* The Jewish value of saving a life. *Piku'ach nefesh* is so important, it supersedes virtually every other commandment in the Torah.

 **inspection:** A check done on vehicles to make sure they are safe to operate.

 **Tiberias:** A city in Israel on the western shore of the Lake Kinneret, also known as Lake Tiberias.